D0501324

The
Chameleon Wore
Chartreuse

The
Chameleon Wore
Chartreuse

FROM THE TATTERED CASEBOOK OF

CHET GECKO
PRIVATE EYE

Bruce Hale

HARCOURT, INC.

San Diego • New York • London

Many thanks to Michael and Steven,
who shared the gecko vision.

Requests for permission to make copies
of any part of the work should be mailed to
the following address:
Permissions Department, Harcourt, Inc.,
6277 Sea Harbor Drive, Orlando, Florida 32887-6777

Library of Congress Cataloging-in-Publication Data
Hale, Bruce.
The chameleon wore chartreuse: from the tattered
casebook of Chet Gecko, private eye/written and
illustrated by Bruce Hale.—1st ed.
p.   cm.
"A Chet Gecko Mystery."
Summary: When hired by a fellow fourth-grader to
find her missing brother, Chet Gecko uncovers
a plot involving a Gila monster's revenge upon
the school football team.
[1. Geckos—Fiction.   2. Lizards—Fiction.   3. Schools—
Fiction.   4. Lost and found possessions—Fiction.
5. Mystery and detective stories.]   I. Title.
PZ7.H1295Ch   2000
[Fic]—dc21   99-50673
ISBN 0-15-202281-3

Text set in Bembo
Display type set in Elroy
Designed by Ivan Holmes

First edition
A C E G H F D B

Printed in the United States of America

For J. C., my first reader, and Mom and Dad, who
introduced me to the low-rent charms of gumshoes

A private message from the private eye . . .

I've always loved a good mystery. Like, how do they squeeze ketchup into those little plastic packets? And, why is cafeteria food so bad? And, who put the *boom* in the *shaka-laka-boom-boom*?

My curiosity has given me a reputation around school. Kids talk. They say I'm someone who can solve mysteries.

They're right. I can.

Who am I?

Chet Gecko—Private Eye.

I go to fourth grade at Emerson Hicky Elementary.

I'm a lizard.

1

The Case of the Long-Gone Lizard

Some cases start rough, some cases start easy. This one started with a dame. (That's what we private eyes call a girl.)

It was a hot day in September. The kind of day when kindergartners wake up cranky from their naps. The kind of day when teachers pull their hair and dream of moving to Antarctica.

In other words, a normal school day.

I was watching a fly. He zigged and zagged over my desk. He flew barrel rolls and loop-de-loops. Near as I could tell, he was getting ready to sing "The Star Spangled Banner."

So I shot out my tongue and zapped him. Bull's-eye. Midmorning snack.

"Nice shot, private eye."

I looked up. She was cute and green and scaly. She looked like trouble and she smelled like... grasshoppers.

Shirley Chameleon leaned on my desk. Her chartreuse scarf tickled my nose.

"Hey, Chet," she said.

"Hey, Shirley," I answered.

"Haven't seen you around for a while," she said. "Where've you been?"

"Duh. Right here in class." I've always been fast with a comeback.

"Listen, I need your help," she said.

I checked out the classroom. Old Man Ratnose was busy grading papers. Tony Newt was scribbling rude designs on Walter Pigeon's tail feathers while his brother stifled giggles. The other students were reading their books or quietly torturing each other. Kids.

"Okay, Shirley," I said. "Let's step into my office."

We walked back behind the aquarium.

"Sit," I said. She sat. She turned a deep brown, to match the chair. Chameleons do that.

"Spill your guts," I said. She spilled.

"It's my little brother, Billy," said Shirley.

I knew the kid. He had Day-Glo stripes and a bad attitude. He liked to light matches off his scales and put them out in his nostrils.

Pretty tough for a first grader.

"What's up with Billy?" I asked Shirley. "Did he steal some kindergartner's lunch money?"

"No, it's not that, it's—oh, never mind." Shirley shook her head and stood up. One tearful eye looked at me while her other eye watched a gnat flying above us. Chameleons do that.

"Yuck, stop it," I said. "Look at me with both eyes."

She did.

"I can't help Billy unless you tell me what's wrong," I said. "I need a lead."

"A what?"

"A lead. A place to start."

She dabbed at her eyes with a handkerchief. I zapped my tongue out and nailed the gnat. No sense in wasting good food. But I almost choked on the bug when she finally answered.

"Billy has disappeared," she said. "He never showed up for school. I found his book bag on the playground, and I—I just know something's wrong." Shirley turned a lovely shade of blue.

She was the kind of girl I could have fallen for. If I liked girls.

"Couldn't Billy be playing hooky?" I said.

"The last time he played hooky without me, I tied his tail into a knot."

I blinked. No wonder Billy had a bad attitude.

"Still, have you checked his usual hangouts?" I said. "You know, the mall, the sandbox, the tattoo parlor?"

"I tried all those places," said Shirley. "No luck. He's gone."

"I wonder where he went," I said.

"Oh, that's great." She pouted. "You're some detective. You're supposed to know these things."

"I'm a detective, not a mind reader," I said.

She grabbed my arm.

"Chet, you've got to find him today, before the football game."

"Why? Has he got the football?" I chuckled.

"It's not funny. My family is coming to the game, and I'm supposed to watch Billy. If he's not there, my mom will kill me."

Shirley shuddered and turned a little green around the gills (or where her gills would've been, if she'd been a fish).

"So, you don't have anything for me to go on?" I said.

"There is one thing," she said. "At breakfast he said he had to meet with someone named Herman." She looked down. "I think Herman's nickname is Monster, or something like that."

Swell. Just swell.

5

The first case of a new school year, and already things were looking bad. The last time Shirley saw her little brother, he was talking about meeting a Gila monster named Herman.

And most first graders would rather spend summer vacation in a box with the bogeyman than spend a few friendly minutes with Herman the Gila Monster.

It was going to be a long day.

2

Sing a Song of Stinkbug Pie

If you've never met a Gila monster, let me tell you: They are tough customers. They're big, strong, and dumb, and they have really bad breath. Seriously. You wouldn't want to kiss one.

Oh, and one other thing: They're poisonous.

Of course, I didn't tell Shirley her little brother had gone to meet a poisonous goon the size of a refrigerator. Instead I said, "Herman, huh? Do any of Billy's little friends know Herman?"

One of Shirley's eyes rolled back as she thought about it. The other eye kept looking at the ground. I shuddered. What a creepy habit.

But then, we geckos lose our tails sometimes, so I guess I shouldn't talk.

"Billy *has* been hanging out with the Rat Sisters lately," she said. "Maybe they'd know about Herman."

The Rat Sisters are a couple of sweet girls who like to pull the wings off flies and make umbrellas with them. With the wings, I mean. I made a note to see the Rat Sisters at lunch.

And thinking of lunch reminded me of my fee.

"Will you take the case?" Shirley asked.

"That depends," I said. "Can you afford me? I get a hundred bucks a day, plus expenses." I had read that in a detective book somewhere.

Shirley coughed. "I can afford fifty cents a day," she said.

"Shirley, you jest," I replied.

Shirley groaned. My stomach grumbled.

"Look," she said. "My dad is a good cook. Maybe I could just feed you lunch for a week."

I raised an eyebrow. "Your *dad*?"

"What's so funny about that? Some of the world's best chefs are men, and—"

"All right, all right, it's a deal," I said.

Shirley beamed. "We're having stinkbug pie for dessert tonight. I'll bring you leftovers tomorrow—if you find Billy in time."

My stomach growled. "I'll get right on the case," I said.

I stood up to go, and stepped around the aquarium. But just then, Old Man Ratnose glared at me from his desk at the front of the room.

Oh yeah. School.

"Chet Gecko, where is your reading book?" he demanded.

"Teacher, it's a mystery to me," I said. Mr. Ratnose bared his front teeth. I whispered to Shirley, "I'll start at recess."

"Oh, thank you, Chet," she said.

She kissed my cheek. Then Shirley turned and wriggled back to her desk.

I wiped the cooties off my cheek. Dames. What's a guy supposed to do?

3

Green Blobs of Fate

The bell rang. Recess. I strolled down the hall to Billy's classroom. Screaming first graders tumbled over each other, racing out the door toward the playground.

They were headed for swings and slides. Those carefree kids.

I had bigger bugs to fry.

I had to get a look at Billy's desk. It could hold a clue to his disappearance—or a wad of forgotten homework and moldy socks.

Only a true detective could tell.

I hid behind a razzleberry bush and waited for the teacher to leave. There she was: the great horned toad, Mrs. Toaden—Old Toady to those who had survived her class.

Years ago kids used to whisper that she rolled in the vats of Jell-O before the cafeteria served it.

Nothing was ever proved. But you couldn't help wondering about the green blobs on her dress.

"Come along, you little runt!" said Mrs. Toaden to a straggling first grader.

"Yes, teacher. I'm coming." The little shrew fumbled with his book bag.

But he wasn't moving fast enough, I guess. She gave him a friendly punt to speed him up. The kid sailed between two of the posts that lined the covered walkway. Field goal.

Sooner or later he would learn. Never stand between a teacher and her Jell-O.

Old Toady trundled off. I eased toward the door, with a wary eye on Mrs. Toaden. Just as I reached for the doorknob, she stopped dead in her tracks and turned around.

Fa-zip! I barely had time to scramble up the wall, out of sight. Sometimes it pays to be a lizard.

Old Toady waddled back to the classroom like a duck on a hot date. She locked the door, then made tracks toward the cafeteria.

I slithered down the wall and tried the knob. Locked tight. Glancing up and down the hallway, I slipped the point of my tail into the keyhole and wiggled it around.

I tried the doorknob again. This time the lock's

tumblers clicked—on my tail. *Ouch!* But the door-knob turned.

I slipped inside and eyeballed the dark classroom. It hadn't changed much in the years since I'd been there. It still smelled of chalk, and fear, and stale graham crackers. I looked out across the rows of pink plastic desks.

Using my incredible powers of detection, I discovered Billy's desk. It was the one with the nametag that read BILLY.

I slid into the seat and checked again to make sure I was alone. I had only a few minutes to search before Old Toady returned.

So far, so good. I opened the desk. *Creeeaak!* I held my breath. Had someone heard? I glanced at the windows, but I was alone. I looked into the desk.

Yuck! Sitting on a stack of papers was a sandwich so old even the cafeteria wouldn't serve it. It looked like a science project on The Wonders of Mold.

I pushed it aside with a pencil. Underneath was a crayon drawing of mutant people.

Or maybe they were broccoli. Whatever Billy was up to, it sure wasn't art lessons.

I dug deeper into the mess. A rubber-band gun . . . a box of nails . . . a hangman's noose . . . a photo of the Loch Ness monster . . . Nothing suspicious here.

Wait a minute! I turned back to the drawing.

It showed a small creature with a tail, beating up a big creature. A girlish blob in the back was saying, "my hiro!" in a word balloon. The big creature was labeled "hurmn," the blob was called "Shrlee," and the small creature's name was "me."

Hmmm. Maybe Billy was planning to rumble with Herman. But why would he try to beat up that big lug? Picking a fight with a Gila monster was about as smart as playing hopscotch on the freeway.

And Herman was no ordinary Gila monster. After all, he'd been booted off the football team for biting a referee's ear and throwing him into the bleachers. How many sixth graders could say that?

I stuck my nose back into Billy's desk. I had to

find out more. Shirley had a stinkbug pie with my name on it, if only I could crack this case.

I dug deeper. I had just spotted something that looked like a map when a familiar sound sent chills down to my tail.

4

Toad Away

"Chester? Chester Gecko!"

I hate when teachers use my full name.

"Old To—uh, I mean, Mrs. Toaden," I said. "What a pleasure."

Mrs. Toaden waddled through the door and over to her desk. She sneered at me.

"Returning to the scene of the crime, eh?"

I perked up. "What crime?"

"Your grades in my class, mister. You were the worst student I've ever had, and I've had quite a few."

"Flattery won't work with me," I said. "It's been tried."

Mrs. Toaden picked up the heavy ruler from her desk and stroked it. My knuckles got nervous, remembering old times.

"So what are you doing back here?" she asked. "Taking William's place? Or do you want to make up some of that homework you never finished?"

"Uh, I'm on a case." Under cover of the desktop, I slipped the map into my pocket. "Maybe you can help me."

"Why should I?" Mrs. Toaden gave me her dead-eyed stare, the one that makes first graders faint. But not me. I was a big, tough, fourth-grade private eye.

"Why should you? Because," I said, "I could tell somebody about a certain teacher's relationship with a certain cool green dessert." I stood up beside the desk.

Old Toady blinked. Her long tongue sneaked out of the corner of her mouth and tidied up some green blobs on her upper lip. If they weren't Jell-O, I didn't want to know what they were.

"Okay, suppose I do want to help you," she said. "What do you want to know?"

"When was the last time you saw Billy?"

"Yesterday, right after school."

"And what was he doing?"

Mrs. Toaden used the ruler to scratch one of her many warts. Her bug eyes wandered.

She has a face that only a mother could love. And horny toads' mothers abandon them at birth.

"William was talking with that boy Herman and one of the other football players."

17

"Which one?"

"All those hedgehogs look alike to me." She croaked loudly. "I think maybe it was Brick."

"Did you hear what they were saying?"

Mrs. Toaden slapped her ruler down on the desk.

"What am I, a tape recorder? Enough questions! You're the hotshot detective; you find out."

I smiled sweetly and edged toward the door. "J-E-L-L-O," I sang.

She blinked again. Blackmail is a many-splendored thing.

"One last question," I said. "Did you get an excuse from Billy's mom today?"

Old Toady snatched a piece of paper off her desk and crumpled it in her scaly fist.

"Yes, a little rat brought it. And you can take comfort in this, Chester: William's mom spells almost as badly as you do!"

She tossed the paper at my face. Purely on reflex, I caught the wad with my tongue. Yuck—perfumed paper.

Curious first graders peeked through the doorway.

"Have a nice day, Chester." Mrs. Toaden growled. "Class dismissed."

I strolled out the door. The first graders melted away.

"Not you, you little rodents!" Old Toady roared. She raised her ruler like a sword. "Get your tails in here!"

Ah, school days, dear old golden rule days. I missed first grade.

Like a case of the mumps.

5

The Messes of Hippopotamia

O n the way back to my own classroom, I un-folded the note Mrs. Toaden had thrown at me. It read:

Pls xcuze Blly frm skool today. He iz sikk.

Hmmm. Billy's mom had the same spelling prob-lems that Billy did. In fact, her handwriting was pretty close to the writing I'd seen on Billy's drawings.

Could Billy have faked his own excuse note? Duh. Of course he had. But why?

And who had brought the note? Was it one of the Rat Sisters?

I pulled the map out of my pocket and unfolded it. Maybe I'd find a clue to where Billy had gone.

But it wasn't a map at all. It looked like a crazy spider had crawled into an inkwell and danced the Funky Chicken across the paper. The sheet was covered with Xs and Os, and arrows and squiggles—almost like a football play.

Maybe it had nothing to do with the case. But it was the only clue I had. I needed to talk with a football player named Brick, and I thought I knew where to find him.

I walked into my own classroom and sat down. Mr. Ratnose started to tell us all about the history of Mesopotamia, or the messes of Hippopotamia—I forget which. I raised my hand.

"Yes?" he asked.

"Mr. Ratnose, can I go to the principal's office?"

He frowned at me.

"No, you may not. Now, please don't interrupt."

Mr. Ratnose kept rattling on about ancient ruins. I gave him thirty seconds, then raised my hand again.

"What is it, Chester?"

"Can I please go to the principal's office?"

"No!" he said. His eyes narrowed. "Now, for the last time, stop interrupting me."

I gave him ten seconds this time. My hand shot up.

His whiskers twitched. "What... is... it... Chester?"

"Can I please—"

"*Absolutely not!* You've interrupted me for the last time!"

Mr. Ratnose scribbled a quick note. He shoved it into my hand.

"Take this note and go straight to the principal's office. Do you understand?"

"Yes, Mr. Ratnose." I walked to the door and turned around. "Oh, Mr. Ratnose? Thanks."

I didn't know for sure that Brick would be in Principal Zero's office, but most of the football team spent half their days there. It was like a game with them. Whoever bugged his teacher the most won an all-expenses-paid trip to the principal's office.

If I'd had a choice, I would have stayed as far away as possible from the three-time winner of the Meanest Principal in the Universe award. But duty called.

And the twisted trail of my case led right to the door of that fat cat, Principal Zero.

6

Thick as a Brick

I entered the administration building. It was a light day. Only a dozen kids sat in the hard chairs outside the principal's office.

And his spanking machine wasn't even turned on.

The secretary didn't look up as I gave her my note. "Take a number, take a seat." She sighed.

I ripped number 187 from the ticket roll and sat down. I sized up my fellow troublemakers. They were carving their names on the chairs, flicking spitballs at each other, and playing punching games.

Pretty quiet for a Friday.

Half of the kids looked like football-team material—wide as refrigerators, but without the little lights inside. I leaned toward one of them.

"Brick?" I said.

"Say what?"

"I'm looking for Brick."

"Ask a building." He laughed, showing teeth as yellow as candy corn.

"He's a football player," I said. "You know, football?"

The light went on behind his eyes.

"Yeah, football good," he said. "Brick over there."

The goon pointed toward the corner with a hand the size of a dinner plate. *Mmm, dinner.* That reminded me: It was almost time for lunch.

I took an empty chair beside a big redheaded hedgehog.

"You're Brick," I said.

"Yeah, so?"

"Chet Gecko, private eye. I want to ask you a few questions."

"What is this, a pop quiz?" he said.

I thought I'd be tricky and try the old switch-eroo.

"You might say that. First question: What is the square root of 369?"

"Uh . . . ," he said.

"Next, what is the capital of Mesopotamia?"

"Hmm," he said.

"And third, when did you last see Billy Chameleon?"

"Billy? Me and Herman was talking with him after school yesterday."

The old switcheroo. It worked every time.

"What were you talking about?" I asked.

"Herman made a joke about some cheerleader. I don't think Billy liked it."

"Why not?" I said.

"I think she was his sister."

Shirley, a cheerleader? That dame was as full of surprises as a toad is full of flies. I wondered what else she hadn't told me.

"Do you remember anything more?"

"That's about it," said Brick. He scratched his neck bristles. "I went to football practice after that."

Football. I remembered the strange drawing in my pocket. I fished it out and showed it to him.

"This mean anything to you?" I said. "Is it a football play?"

He squinted at the paper and turned it around in his hands.

"Number 184!" said the secretary.

"That's me," he said. "Gotta go."

"Wait. What about that drawing?"

"Hah! Whoever drew this was some lame football player."

"Why's that?" I asked.

"It looks like the crowd is playing and the football teams ain't."

He wadded up the paper and tossed it at me.

What did I look like, a trash can? I was going to have to start dressing better.

7

Big Fat Zero

While Brick got his tongue-lashing from Principal Zero, I puzzled. This case had more unanswered questions than a five-hour math test.

Where was Billy? What did Herman have to do with his disappearance? Why hadn't Shirley told me she was a cheerleader?

And what the heck was "osmosis"? (I needed to learn that for Monday's science quiz.)

I puzzled until the secretary called out, "Number 187!"

I got up, turned the knob, and stepped into the principal's office. Behind the desk sat the enormous Mr. Zero. Big Fat Zero, the kids called him. But never to his face.

"Come in, Mr. Gecko," he purred.

I shut the door. Principal Zero picked up the note Mr. Ratnose had written. He stroked his whiskers.

"So you've been giving poor Mr. Ratnose a hard time, eh?" he asked. "Why did you disrupt his class?"

"I just wanted to come to the principal's office."

Mr. Zero eyed me suspiciously. "You wanted to come here? What for?"

"Just wanted to say, Have a nice weekend."

"That can't be it," he said.

"Oh yeah. That's it. Have a nice weekend, Principal Zero."

His eyes narrowed. He sharpened his claws on the office drapes. They looked pretty ragged, like he'd done it a time or two before.

"I know you're up to something," he said. "And I don't like your attitude."

"Neither do I," I said. "It's pretty bad. I stay up late at night worrying about it."

Principal Zero ground his teeth. His tail twitched. He looked scarier than a grumpy parent on report-card day. But he had nothing on me.

"I'm letting you go this time, young Gecko," he said. "But watch your step. I've got my eye on you."

I slipped out the door before he could change his mind. On the way back to class, I reviewed what I had so far on this case.

Absolutely nothing.

Without a break, I'd never find Billy before the football game. My stomach whimpered.

If things didn't start looking up, I'd have to ask for help. But first I wanted to put the squeeze on Shirley. She was holding out on me, and I had to know why.

I stepped into Mr. Ratnose's class. His nerves were ragged. I could tell because it was quiet-reading time again. Once a day was normal. Two reading periods meant my teacher had a headache. Three times meant he was on the edge of a breakdown.

I eased into the chair behind Shirley and opened a book.

I scrawled a quick note and slipped it to her. It said: *Why didn't you tell me you're a cheerleader?*

She stamped her foot and wrote back:

It has nothing to do with the case, and it's none of your business, anyway!

Is so! I wrote. I was good with comebacks. *And how do you know Herman the Gila Monster?*

Shirley started to write something, then scribbled it out. She wrote again and slipped me another note:

Wouldn't it be easier to talk? Why are we writing notes?

They always do this in spy movies, I wrote back.

Shirley sighed and turned in her chair. She whispered out of the corner of her mouth, "Chet, Herman caught me doing—I'd rather not say. Look, I hired you to find my brother. Why are you sticking your nose into my business?"

"Your business may be connected to your brother's disappearance," I said. "I've got a hunch Herman's up to something, and Billy's involved."

"Well, hurry up and find him," she said. "I'll be dead meat if he's not at that football game."

And I knew what that would mean: Bye-bye, stinkbug pie.

8

Rats for Lunch

When the lunch bell rang, I scooted out the door. I wanted to catch the Rat Sisters before they started stealing little kids' lunches. If they were hungry, I could pump some information from them. I leaned against a trash can and waited. It didn't take long.

"Hey, Nadine. Hey, Rizzo," I said. "Guess what? It's National Take-a-Doofus-to-Lunch Day, so I thought I'd share a sandwich with you."

"Very funny, Gecko," said the bigger one, Rizzo.

The Rat Sisters make the Wicked Witch of the West look like a Girl Scout. The only thing they like more than bullying smaller kids is pigging out on food—any food. I had just what they wanted.

I pulled a peanut butter-and-ladybug sandwich from my lunch bag. Both rats stared at it, hypnotized.

"So," I said. "I hear you girls hang out with Billy Chameleon."

"Yeah, sometimes," said Nadine. "What's it to you? Are you his boyfriend?"

I moved the sandwich to the right. Their eyes went right. I moved it to the left. Their eyes went left.

"Have you seen Billy today?" I asked.

"Not since—no," said Rizzo. "Hey are you going to eat that sandwich, or just dance with it?"

"Well, I might share, if you'll share information," I said.

"Like what?" said Nadine.

"Like, did you take Billy's excuse note to Old Toady? Like, where is Billy right now?" I said.

"Yeah, I gave her that note. He's—" Nadine began.

"Cool it, Brillo Whiskers," said her sister.

"You're the Brillo Whiskers," said Nadine.

"You were about to spill the beans. The Big Guy wouldn't like that." Rizzo bared her teeth and glared at her sister.

"Was not," said Nadine, glaring back, eyeball-to-eyeball.

I dangled the sandwich above them.

"Why wouldn't the Big Guy want me to know anything?" I said.

They both looked up at the sandwich. I waited.

"No way, Gecko," said Rizzo. "You can't bribe us that easy."

Suddenly Nadine pointed past my shoulder, across the playground.

"Uh-oh," she said. "Now we're in trouble."

I looked. Nobody there but kids eating lunch. I turned back. My lunch was bounding over the grass, held fast in the grubby paws of two running Rat Sisters.

"Nice try, private eye," Nadine shouted over her shoulder. "If you want a clue, ask the Big Baboo."

Rizzo added, "Or answer this: What do you get when you cross a duck with a trash collector?"

I watched my lunch disappear, and I wondered if I could convince Shirley to pay me in advance. My stomach wondered, too.

9

To Grill a Mockingbird

"What do you get when you cross a duck with a trash collector?" I asked myself. "Grease and quackers? No, that's not it. A trash can that flies? Nawww..."

This was one tricky clue. And who the heck was the Big Baboo? I knew I needed help. And I knew where to turn.

Across the playground, under a shady tree, sat Natalie Attired. She was a good friend. Natalie was also the smartest mockingbird around, and she never let anyone forget it.

"Hiya, Chet!" she said. "Care for a worm?"

She held out her lunch bag. Normally I prefer bugs. But my stomach said yes before my mouth

could say no. I snatched a worm and chomped into it. Kind of rubbery.

"So what's shaking, Mr. Detective?" said Natalie.

"Mmm-hma-vhmph," I mumbled around the worm.

"Chasing some bad guys?"

"Mmmf, you might say that," I finally said. "Hey, Natalie, I—uh, I need your, uh—that is…"

"Ha!" she laughed. "'Natalie, I—uh, I need your, uh—that is…'" Natalie made her voice sound even more like me than I did.

"Hey, cut that out!" I said.

" 'Hey, cut that out!' " she echoed in my voice. My eyes narrowed. "Natalie—"

"All right, all right," she said in her normal voice. "I'm a mockingbird. Sometimes I mock." Natalie cocked her head. "So what were you trying to say before I interrupted?"

I took a breath and tried to start again. "Well, um, you see—"

Natalie's eyes lit up. "Wait, don't tell me," she said. "You've found a clue you can't crack, so you want to borrow my brainpower."

I hate it when she's right. I tried to slip the rest of the worm back into her lunch bag. It limped away. I let it.

"Yeah." I sighed. "I need your help. What do you say?"

"Sure, I'll help you," she said. "But on one condition: If I solve your clue, you take me along when you investigate."

"But I'm a private *I*," I said. "Not a private *we*. All the best private eyes work alone."

"Okay," she said. "Fine with me. Solve it yourself." Natalie fluffed her feathers and poked her beak back into her lunch bag.

I swallowed my pride, along with the last bits of worm.

"All right, it's a deal," I said. I told her about Shirley's missing brother and showed her the strange drawing I'd found in Billy's desk.

"Hmm," Natalie said. She cocked her head. "Can't solve this without more information."

"Some help *you* are."

"Have you dug up anything else so far?" Natalie asked. She slurped another fat, juicy worm.

I looked away. Then I told her about the mysterious Big Baboo and the riddle that the Rat Sisters had given me.

Natalie laughed. "Man, don't you ever read joke books? I don't know any Big Baboo, but that other clue is so easy, I almost feel guilty."

"Oh yeah?" I said. "If you're so smart, what do you get when you cross a duck with a trash collector?"

"Down in the dumps," she said.

I smacked my forehead. The dumps! Of course —maybe Herman had dragged Billy to the city dump to beat him up. Or worse.

"That was so easy," I said. "Why didn't I think of it?"

Thankfully Natalie didn't answer me. She preened her feathers while a sly look came over her face.

"That's why every detective needs a partner," she said.

"Partner?! I never said you could be my partner."

"We'll talk about it on the way to the dump," said Natalie.

10

Cheers Looking at You, Kid

As we were heading across the playground, I noticed a group of girls (a giggle of girls?) over by the gym. I looked closer. Shirley was with them.

"Hang on a minute," I said to Natalie. "Before we check out the dump, I've got to do a little shadowing."

"Shadowing?" said Natalie. "Oh, goody. I love to make shadow animals. Did I ever show you my bunny rabbit?"

I gave her my deadpan stare. "Enough with the wisecracks."

"Polly wanna wisecracker?" Natalie's bright birdy eyes twinkled. "Sorry. So who are we shadowing?"

"Shirley Chameleon."

"You're following your client around?" said
Natalie. "Why? Are you in love with her?"

I grabbed Natalie by her tail feathers and twisted.
"Take that back," I said. "Private eyes don't go for
mushy stuff."

"Ow!" Natalie hopped from foot to foot. "Okay,
okay, I take it back."

I let her go. Natalie rubbed her tail feathers. "So
you're not in love with Shirley," she said. "But how
come you're following your client instead of the
suspects?"

"She's holding out on me. I can feel it. She
knows about some link between Herman and Billy,
and she won't tell me."

Natalie and I looked over at the girls. Two football players joined the group, and the girls giggled
even louder. Why is it that jocks make girls twitter?
They never twitter for private eyes.

Not that I would want them to. Yuck.

"So what's the plan, Stan?" said Natalie.

"Time to play a little I Spy," I said. "Come on."

We strolled past the swings, then ducked behind
some bushes and sneaked toward the gym. As we
edged along the wall, just around the corner from
the group, I raised a hand.

"Up," I whispered, and pointed to the gymna-
sium roof.

Natalie flapped to the rooftop, and I climbed the wall. I figured Shirley and the girls might not notice us if we came in from above. As I crawled closer to the corner, the voices and laughter grew louder below me.

"Oh, Brick, you're just the funniest thing," a girl said.

"Not half as funny as that goofy gecko in your class," he said. Brick snorted and giggled, a sound like two owls in a blender.

"Who does he think he is?" he said. "With the detective getup and everything? He couldn't detect a football if it hit him on the head."

I stifled a snarl. Brick should talk. He couldn't detect his nose with two fingers up his nostrils. I peeked carefully around the corner.

"Oh, he's not that bad," said Shirley quietly.

Hoots and laughter greeted her remark. "Ooo, Shir-ley's in lo-ove, Shir-ley's in lo-ove," chanted a couple of mynah birds.

Natalie looked down at me and smirked.

"Am not!" said Shirley.

"And I thought you liked *Herman!*" said a sassy mouse, Frenchy LaTrine.

"I don't, either!" said Shirley. "You guys are so thick!" She turned brick red and flounced off with her tail in a tangle.

I glanced at Natalie. I mouthed, "She likes Herman?"

Natalie shrugged. I turned back to the conversation.

"So are you cheerleaders doing something special at the pep rally today?" said the other football player, an armadillo with a cauliflower nose.

"You bet!" said Frenchy. Her tail swung in a circle. "Just wait until you see our routine with the Big Baboo—it'll knock your pads off!"

The Big Baboo! Sometimes a private eye gets lucky. I looked down at Shirley, who was wriggling across the playground. I looked back at the cheerleaders.

Stay, or follow Shirley? I decided to stay.

"Don't forget, Frenchy," said one of the mynahs. "We've got cheer practice next period in the gym."

"Okey-dokey!" said Frenchy the mouse. I had the feeling she always talked in exclamation points. Cheerleaders.

"Don't you love the part when we—" she started to say.

"Hey, Chet!" shouted a loud voice. "What are you doing up there?"

It was my sister, Pinky. The littlest first grader, with the biggest mouth.

"Shhh!" I said. She didn't take the hint.

"You know Mom told you never to climb on school buildings."

I shushed her again, but Pinky planted her fists on her skinny green hips. "I'm telling! I'm telling so bad," she said.

The other kids looked up at me and laughed. My cover was blown.

"Hey, look!" said Brick. "It's Super Gecko! Able to climb tall buildings with a single slither! Able to munch huge bugs with a single slurp!"

The armadillo joined in, "Yeah, and the only thing that can stop him is his archenemy, Baby-Sister Girl!"

They laughed until they snorted. This made the cheerleaders giggle even harder. I clammed up. A private eye has his dignity, after all.

I scrambled to the roof and stood beside Natalie. Pinky stuck out her tongue. "I'm telling Mom!" she shouted again.

"You do and you die, cockroach breath!" I said. Even a private eye's patience has limits. "Come on, Natalie."

I led the way over the back wall of the gym. Natalie floated lazily down beside me.

"To the dumps?" she asked.

"My reputation's gone there already. But before

we join it, I've got some questions for the Big Baboo."

Natalie chuckled. "Anything you say, Super Gecko."

"Ah, shut up, Wonder Bird," I said.

11

Never Trust a Hungry Rat

Natalie and I slipped through the door into the gym. It stank of sweat, sneakers, and humiliating defeat in basketball.

Or maybe that was just me.

A couple of sixth graders were shooting hoops at the far end. Otherwise the building was deserted. We strolled over to the basketball players, a burly seagull and a snake.

"Hey, sports fans," I said. "Is either of you the Big Baboo?"

They stopped playing. The seagull's mouth twisted into a sneer and her chest puffed out. "Do I look like a big baboo?" she said.

"Beats me," I said. "That's what I'm trying to find out."

"Sonny, I'm a potentate of poobah," she said.

"What about you?" I asked the snake.

He coiled up lazily.

"He's a grand funkmeister," said the seagull. "But neither of us is a big baboo."

"Ah, I see," I said. Actually, I didn't.

"Can you tell us where to find the Big Baboo?" Natalie asked the snake. His forked tongue flickered.

"Hey, your guess is as good as ours," said the seagull. She stabbed a grimy wing feather toward the opposite wall. "Try the coach's office."

I glanced at the silent snake. "Tell me something," I asked the seagull, "does he ever talk?"

"Nah," she said. "But he's got a killer jump shot."

Natalie and I turned and headed for the coach's office. Coach "Beef" Stroganoff knows everyone who uses the gym. He'd know the Big Baboo.

I rapped on the glass of his half-open door. "Coach Stroganoff? Can we talk?"

Inside, a massive groundhog sat snoring in his chair, hind paws up on the desk. A little string of drool dangled from the corner of his mouth. Coach Stroganoff: man of action.

A sly smile twisted Natalie's beak. "Oh, Coach Stroganoff," she said in Mrs. Toaden's voice. "You're so big and strong. Can you help me?"

The coach's feet hit the floor. He came awake,

shaking his head and flinging off the drool. "Beulah, honey?" he muttered. "Is that you?"

Coach Stroganoff and Beulah Toaden, eh? I'd have to remember that one.

"No, Coach, it's us," I said.

The coach's sleepy gaze swung to me. "Chet Gecko?" he said. "Don't you owe me some push-ups?"

"Oh, uh . . . no, Coach. You must have me confused with my evil twin."

He grunted suspiciously.

"Coach, we're looking for the Big Baboo," said Natalie. "Can you help us?"

He blinked slowly and scratched his nose. "The Big Baboo? Why do you want the Big Baboo?"

"I want to talk with him . . . or her," I said.

He stared at me while a smile slowly stretched the corners of his mouth. Coach Stroganoff chuckled, a sound like a bullfrog belching in a barrel.

"You want to talk to the Big Baboo?" he said. "Well, you're welcome to try. But your conversation may be a little one-sided."

He lumbered to his feet and pushed open the equipment room door. The small space was jammed with jump ropes, balls, and exercise mats.

In a tall case by the wall stood a statue of our team mascot, the Golden Gopher. It looked pretty goofy to me, but it meant a lot to the school. No accounting for taste.

"Find your friend yet?" said Coach Stroganoff. He smirked.

I stepped deeper into the room and looked around. A dark shape caught my eye. Slumped among the bats and balls was a big, stuffed dummy. It looked like a huge monkey, the mascot of our rival school, Petsadena Elementary.

And hanging around its neck was a sign that read BIG BABOO.

12

The Dogged Detective

Coach Beef Stroganoff's laughter chased us out of the gym. I leaned against the outside wall. If geckos had ears, steam would have been shooting out of mine.

"Rats!" I said. "They tricked me, those rotten Rat Sisters! They slipped me a red herring."

"A red herring, eh?" said Natalie. "I'd like a couple of those, marinated in olive oil."

"No, you ding-dong," I said. "They gave me a false lead. A dead end. And I wasted precious time on it. How long before the bell rings?"

Natalie glanced at the clock on the gym wall. "Not long," she chirped.

We might have just enough time to make it to

the dump and back before lunch period ended. It would be close, but a private eye lives for danger.

I snagged my skateboard from the bush where I always stash it. We took off.

Five minutes later, I hopped off my skateboard outside the fence. Natalie landed on a nearby stump.

"Why wouldn't you carry me?" I said. "I've never flown before."

"And you won't fly with me," she said. "You are one heavy gecko, Chet. You should lay off the deep-fried termites."

Termites. *Mmm,* that reminded me, I still hadn't eaten lunch. My stomach groaned.

We entered the gate. The dump stretched all around us, as far as the nose could smell. Hills and valleys of old tires, leftover dinners, fat cockroaches, and plain old junk covered the ground.

A shack leaned on the fence like a lovesick walrus on a rock. Inside, a mangy dog snoozed on the floor.

"Hey, mister," I said. "We need some information."

The dog opened one eye. Probably the biggest workout he'd had all day.

"What do I look like, the public library?" he said. "You want information, answer my riddles first."

"Fire away," I said. "I'm a detective."

"What kind of dog likes air conditioning?"

"Umm . . . ," I said.

"A hot dog!" said Natalie.

"Not bad," said the dog. He raised his head and scratched at a flea. "Okay, what is the most expensive dog?"

"Hmm . . . ," I said.

"A golden retriever!" said Natalie.

The mangy dog sat up and smiled, his wet tongue hanging out. "You're good," he said. "One more: What does Lassie use to make her dog biscuits?"

"Well . . . ," I said.

"Collie flour!" said Natalie.

The dog wagged his tail and knocked over a stack of tin cans. "You sure know your dogs," he said. "Now, what can I help you with?"

Natalie grinned at me. I snorted, "Hmph." Then I told him about the missing chameleon, Billy.

"Sure, I saw him earlier," he said. "He and this big guy were arguing. The big guy pushed him around, then they left with an old wig, a wiggly bag, and a pigskin."

"Eeeww," said Natalie.

"Was the pig still inside the skin?" I asked.

The dog snorted. "Don't you young pups know anything? A pigskin is what we called a football, back when I was the fastest halfback around."

"Enough chin waggling, Pops. No time for a side trip down memory lane," I said. "Where did Billy and Herman go when they left here?"

"Look, noodlehead," he said. "You're the detective. You figure it out."

The dog closed his eyes and went back to sleep. A distant bell rang—lunch period was over!

We beat feet. I glanced longingly at the juicy cockroaches as we raced out the gate. Lunch would have to wait.

"Billy and Herman left together?" said Natalie.

I jumped on my skateboard and pushed off. "Maybe he's forcing Billy to help him do something.

And if I know my Gila monsters, Herman is up to no good."

"Sounds like Billy is in trouble," said Natalie, flapping just ahead of me.

"Yeah," I said. "And we'll be in trouble, too, if Ms. Glick catches us."

Gila monsters were one thing. But Ms. Glick, the Beast of Room 3, was another kind of trouble altogether.

13

The Beast of Room 3

Natalie and I flew back to school. Well, actually, she flew. I skateboarded. Coming up the hill, she said, "Good thing I was there, eh?"

"You weren't too bad," I said.

"See, I told you a private eye needs a partner."

"We'll talk about it later," I said. "Right now, we have bigger problems."

At the school gate stood Ms. Glick. She looked meaner than a plateful of lima beans, and uglier than the first day of school after vacation.

Her sharp teeth glinted in a smile.

"Well, well," she said. "Looks like a tardy slip for Miss Natalie. And as for you, Chester Gecko..."

I hate it when they use my full name.

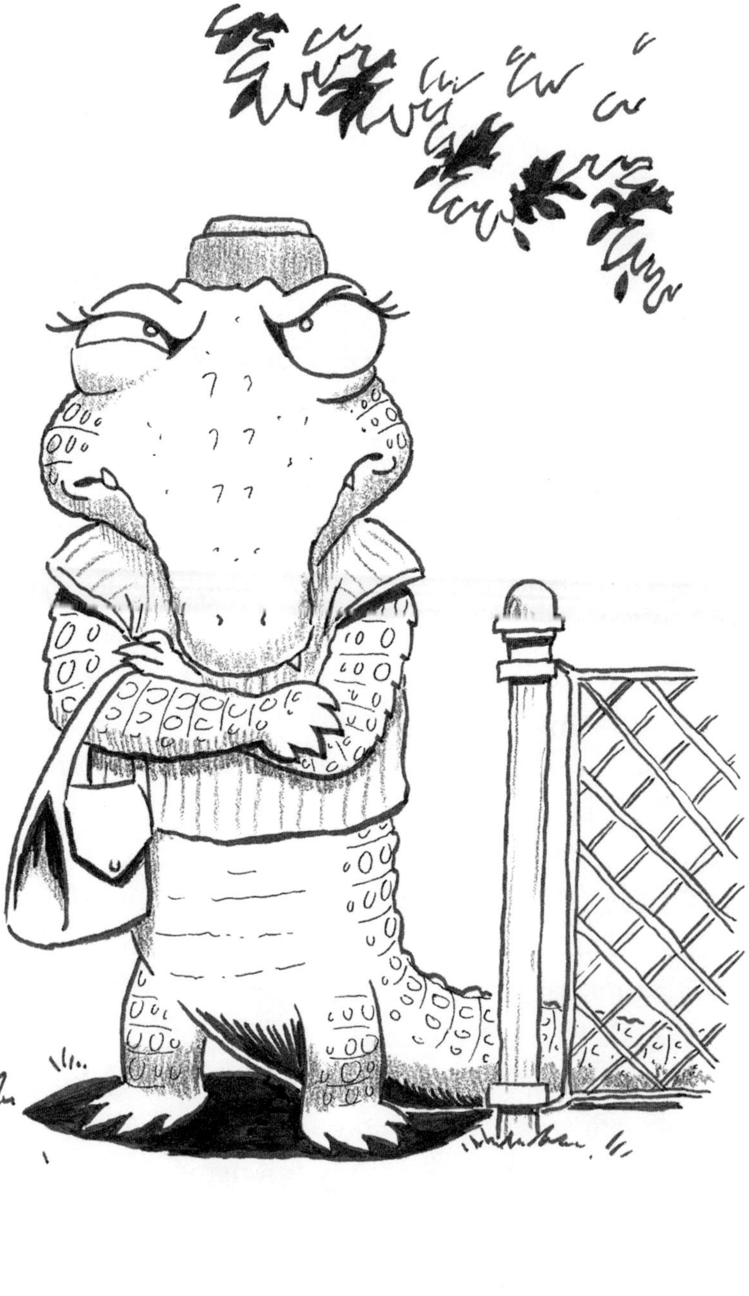

"You'll stay in detention with me and miss the football game after school," said the Beast of Room 3. She chuckled. Then Ms. Glick plunged a scaly paw into her purse, grabbed a pen, and scrawled two pink slips. It hurt. But a private eye never shows pain.

I took the detention slip. "See you later, alligator," I said.

Her jaws snapped shut with a click. "Sassing a teacher," she snarled. "That's another day's detention. Want to try for three days?"

I decided my wit had punished her enough. I clammed up.

Natalie sighed and walked on.

I went to class.

A surprise awaited me there. Sitting on top of my desk was a chocolate-covered termite. A treat! I zapped out my tongue and snagged it. A yummy appetizer. But what a strange aftertaste.

I reached into my mouth and found that a piece of paper had come with the bug. Carefully I peeled it off my tongue and unfolded the soggy paper.

Dear Chet, it read, *I know who you're looking for. I can help.*

Who had written this? It obviously wasn't Shirley. I raised my head and scanned the classroom. But nobody winked, or made a secret hand sign, or shouted out, "It was me!"

I sighed.

It isn't always easy being a detective.

I returned to the note. It continued: *In ten minutes, ask the teacher for permission to get a drink of water. I'll be waiting by the water fountain.*

It was signed, *A friend.*

I sat up straighter. A friend was willing to help me. Things were finally looking up. I might solve this case yet.

I made it through the next ten minutes without Mr. Ratnose calling on me. At the proper time, I raised my hand.

"Mr. Ratnose, can I go get a drink of water?"

He just grunted and waved his hand. I suspected he was glad to see me leave. I scooted down the hall.

Waiting there by the drinking fountain, a pink ribbon in her mousy brown hair, was Frenchy LaTrine.

"Frenchy?!" I said.

"You were expecting maybe Mata Hairy?" she said.

I groaned.

"Chet, we don't have much time!" said Frenchy. Her nose twitched. "I know you're looking for Billy Chameleon. And I know Herman's got him!"

"Is that all?" I said. "I know that already."

"There's more! I overheard Herman at lunch." She glanced over her shoulder and lowered her voice. "He was talking about getting 'sweet' something. I think he's planning to break into the cafeteria!"

I nodded at her. "Thanks, Frenchy. You done good."

She smiled from ear to fuzzy ear, and I turned to go. But then a thought struck me.

"Frenchy? Why are you helping me?"

She pouted. "That Herman! He's such a mean boy—I want to see him get what he deserves!"

"And why did you leave the chocolate-covered termite on my desk?"

Frenchy grinned. "A day without chocolate is like a day without sunshine! And a day without sunshine is like . . . night."

"Mm-hmm," I grunted.

She fiddled with her bow and looked down at her feet. "Chet, a cheerleader's more than just a cute uniform and backflips, you know." Frenchy looked up and batted her eyes. "A cheerleader has a heart, too."

Dames. Who could understand them? I trotted back to the classroom before she could try to kiss me. I'd had enough cooties for one day.

So Herman was planning some stunt in the cafeteria, eh? Well, he hadn't reckoned with Chet Gecko, private eye—defender of casseroles, champion of cupcakes.

There was just one small problem: To reclaim my missing chameleon, I had to get past a Gila monster who made Darth Vader look like a choir boy.

14

Countdown to a Showdown

All afternoon, while Old Man Ratnose talked, I thought about Billy and the Gila monster. I wondered: Were they really going to steal food? What was in the wiggling sack they took from the dump?

And would I ever get to eat lunch?

At break time, Shirley slithered up to me. She blinked her big green eyes.

"Well?" she asked. "Have you found my brother yet?"

"Um . . . hot on his trail," I answered. "Why, I've got all sorts of clues."

"Oh yeah? Like what?" Shirley frowned suspiciously.

I told her about Billy's trip to the dump with Herman, and about what Frenchy had overheard.

"So you see, I'll just slip out after the bell rings and catch them at the cafeteria," I said.

"But Billy wouldn't hang out with Herman." She turned icy blue and stamped her foot. "Stop wasting time on that Gila monster and find my brother!"

"Don't worry, I will." I hoped.

"*Hmph!*" she said. "You're as clueless as a duck in a disco! And there's only one period left!"

She tossed her head and pranced back to her desk.

I looked at the facts of the case. She had a point. Number 1, I hadn't found her brother yet, and time was running short. Number 2, I didn't have a clue how all my clues added up. And number 3, I would be spending the next two days in detention.

I was really making some progress. Any more of this progress, and I could consider a career as a bathroom monitor.

Last period dragged by. When the bell rang, all the other kids ran screaming out to the football field for a pep rally.

I thought maybe Ms. Glick wouldn't miss me too much if I skipped detention—just this once. I plunged into a knot of third graders and tried to blend in. With luck, I could make it to the cafeteria undiscovered.

I bent lower as the group swept past Room 5, past Room 4. Freedom was waiting up ahead. And the end of the case was so close, I could almost taste that stinkbug pie. I bent lower still as we rushed past the dreaded Room 3.

Almost there. And then I sensed kids changing direction.

I kept my head down and my feet flying—and ran headfirst into what felt like a brick wall. I rubbed my head and looked. It was a brick wall with big scaly feet and hangnails!

"Hello, Chester," said Ms. Glick. "Nice of you to join us."

Nice of you to run off and join the zoo, I thought. But I didn't say that. The Beast of Room 3 clamped her jaw down on my coat collar and carried me into detention hall like an old sack lunch.

She dumped me behind a desk. I slumped in my seat. Now how would I get free to solve the case in time?

I looked around the room. The pride of the school surrounded me: A dim-witted toad named Willie. A loudmouthed mynah bird named Amy.

And the two Rat Sisters.

My, my.

15

Detention Ain't for Sissies

The Beast made me write *I will not be a tardy gecko* until I filled up the chalkboard. While I wrote, my back was turned to the Rat Sisters. I listened to their whispers.

"I can't believe we're missing it," said Rizzo. "Herman's big revenge is happening, and we're stuck here in detention."

I leaned back to listen, and kept writing.

"I'd like to see the look on their faces when they—" Nadine stopped.

"Get an earful, Gecko?" said Rizzo.

"What?" I asked. I looked around innocently. She pointed to the blackboard, where I'd written *I will not miss Herman's big revenge*.

I will not be a tardy ge
I will not be a tardy gec
I will not be a tardy geck
I will not be a tardy gecko
I will not be

Oops.

Nadine's whiskers bristled. "Keep your nose out of our business," she said. "If you don't want to lose it."

"Shhh!" said Ms. Glick, from her desk.

"Where's Billy?" I whispered. "Where's that chameleon?"

"Aww," said Nadine. "Didn't the Big Baboo tell you anything?"

I clenched my fist. "I'll 'Big Baboo' you!"

"Cool your jets, Gecko," said Rizzo. "Don't

worry about that chameleon. It's like the farmer said when he lost the butter."

"What's that?"

"It'll churn up," she said. The Rat Sisters giggled.

"That's enough," said Ms. Glick. "I'm going to separate you girls. And, Chester, you will erase that board and write one hundred times, 'I will zip my lip while I'm being punished.'"

I sighed. If my luck continued, I'd be the detention champ of fourth grade. And I was so hungry, I could almost eat the chalk.

Just then the loudspeaker squawked. Principal Zero's menacing purr cut through the static. "Calling Ms. Glick, calling Ms. Glick. This is your pimpernel speaking."

Ms. Glick glanced sharply at the loudspeaker.

The deep voice coughed. "I mean, this is your principal," it said. "Come to my office right now, Ms. Glick. Alone!"

The Beast of Room 3 blushed.

"I want to *talk* to you," said the voice, "in my office."

Ms. Glick frowned. "But—" she said.

"Right now, Glick. Get the lead out!" the voice commanded.

Ms. Glick jumped. She looked at us students, then back at the loudspeaker. She stood up.

"All of you, stay here," said the Beast. She pointed a claw at us. "And you'd better behave." Ms. Glick hustled out the door, thick tail dragging behind her.

I looked at the Rat Sisters. They looked blankly back at me. What was going on?

I edged toward the half-open windows, seeking a sneaky way out. A dark shape ducked behind the bushes outside. I stepped to the window and saw . . . Natalie!

"What are you doing?" I hissed.

"A pretty good imitation of our principal," she whispered. "Want to hear it again?"

I glanced back at the other kids in detention. They were shooting spitwads and chasing each other around the desks.

Natalie threw her voice, and again the loudspeaker squawked. "Attention, students in detention!" growled Principal Zero's voice. "You'd better not try any funny business while Ms. Glick is in my office."

At his words, the kids cowered. They sat down meekly.

"And another thing," said the loudspeaker voice. "Chet Gecko, report to my office immediately, for top-secret, double-Dutch detention. You've been a very naughty gecko."

I tossed a withering glance at the shape behind

the bushes. Then I hotfooted it out the door. Natalie joined me in the hall.

"Pretty good, huh?" she said. "It's handy having a mockingbird for a partner, isn't it?"

I shook my head. "I never said you were my partner."

"You will," she said. "Let's go!"

We shot down the hall, away from Ms. Glick's room. If she caught me, I'd be in detention until I was a grown-up. But I had a chameleon to find and a case to solve.

And a stinkbug pie to eat.

Danger may be my business, but dessert is my delight.

16

Nothing Would Be Finer than to Catch 'Em at the Diner

Natalie and I raced along the empty halls.

"So, what's the plan?" she said. "Where's Billy?"

"The cafeteria!" I said. "Frenchy LaTrine tipped me off. She said Herman was going to get 'sweet' something at the cafeteria. Adding that to what the Rat Sisters said, I know what he's after."

"What?"

"It's 'sweet revenge'! He's going to steal something from the cafeteria."

I panted heavily as we trotted along. Maybe I did need to ease off of those fried termites. . . . Nah. We rounded the last classroom and reached the cafeteria.

I tried the doors. Locked. I peered inside. Deserted.

"Let's check the other side," said Natalie.

The kitchen door was locked, too. I thought about picking the lock with my tail, but something stopped me. The building was as quiet as a classful of kids who don't want to be called on.

Something was wrong.

"Another red herring?" said Natalie.

"No, thanks, I'd rather have stinkbug pie," I said. "But I won't get to eat it unless we figure out where Billy is, pronto." I leaned against the door.

"Hey, Chet, I just thought of something," said Natalie. "Herman wants revenge, right?"

"Right."

Natalie cocked her head. "Why would he want revenge on the cafeteria? What did it ever do to him?"

I scratched my head. "You're right. Those cafeteria ladies let him eat as much as he wants."

"So who *does* Herman have a grudge against?" she said.

Suddenly, the lightbulb went on in the fridge of my brain. I tossed my hat up.

"Natalie, I'm a genius!"

"Compared to whom?" she said.

I clapped her on the shoulder. "I figured it out! Herman wants revenge for being kicked off the football team, so he's going to pull something nasty at the game."

"That's it!" said Natalie. "But how does Billy fit in?"

"*Hmm,*" I said. I picked up my hat. "Beats me."

Natalie squawked. "Wait, don't you see? Herman needs a hand. He's blackmailed Billy into helping him." She took off. "Come on, let's go!"

I jogged along behind her. "Natalie! Where are we going?"

"I don't know," she said.

"What do you mean, you don't know?"

We hustled onto the playground.

"Wait, we can't just keep running," I said. "We've got to figure out where they are."

"Well, duh," she said. "So where could they be—inside the gym? Behind the bleachers? In the parking lot?"

We started across the grass toward the gym. "Slow down and let me think," I said. "Football players... football players..."

Suddenly it hit me.

"Wait, Natalie!" I said. "That funny drawing I found in Billy's desk. It's Herman's plan for wrecking the football game."

We stopped beside the gym and I fished out the drawing. Now it made sense. Sort of.

The *X*s and *O*s were the football players. The *M* was... I didn't know what the *M* was. And the *Z*s were Herman and his friends coming out from under the bleachers, onto the field.

"Natalie, we've got to get out to the football field. They're attacking the team from underneath the bleachers."

Natalie just stared at me with an odd expression on her face.

"Chet," she said. "I have a funny feeling."

"That's what happens when you eat worms for lunch."

She shook her head and pointed behind me.

Something big stepped around the corner. I could tell because the sun went out. I smelled something like funky old sweatsocks dipped in rotten eggs.

I turned around.

"Looking for me?" asked Herman the Gila Monster.

17

He Ain't Heavy, He's My Monster

I looked up at the Gila monster. He wasn't so big. Just twice as tall as me. He wasn't so wide. Just wider than an ice-cream truck.

And he seemed friendly. He showed me all his white fangs in a big grin.

"Looking for me, peeper?" he asked again.

"Well, actually, I'm looking for Billy." The day was sunny, but my knees knocked together. "Have you seen him?"

Herman grinned wider. "Billy?" he said. "Search me."

"Well, if you see him, let me know," I said. "His sister is worried."

Natalie and I started backing away from Herman. We weren't scared. Just careful.

"See you later," said Natalie. We backed up some more and bumped into the Rat Sisters.

"Boss, these guys know too much," said Rizzo.

"No, we don't," I said. "I flunked my last history quiz."

They weren't buying it.

I sighed. "So what are you up to, anyway?"

The Gila monster grinned again. His mouth was a dentist's dream—if you could fix those crooked teeth without losing several fingers.

"Heh-heh-heh," he chuckled. "I got something on you, Chet Gecko. But I promise I not tell, if someone keeps her bargain."

"Enough about me," I said. "Let's talk about you. What are you planning for that football game?"

Herman scratched his knobby head while a thought crossed his mind. It was a long trip.

"No dice, Gecko. You will try stop us if I tell."

"How about a hint?" said Natalie.

Herman looked down at her. "Silly bird, we have fun with football players," he said. "Kickoff is first surprise. Then our little friends."

Natalie looked at me. I raised an eyebrow. Of course—that wriggling sack from the dump. That must be the "little friends."

"When we done, even mascot will wish it never been born." Herman chuckled. "Game will be ruined. Coach will cry."

"Tell the truth," I said. "Aren't you just a little bit sore that they kicked you off the football team?"

The Gila monster growled. "Enough smart talk, Gecko. We tie you up now, so you not spoil fun."

I nodded at Natalie. She dodged one way, I dodged the other. But the Rat Sisters blocked our escape. Herman snatched one of us in each huge fist.

"Gotcha!" he said. "Now hold still, unless you want love bite? . . ."

I eyed his poisonous fangs and shook my head.

Herman grunted. "Bright boy. Bring rope, Rizzo."

Herman carried us to the swimming pool. He sat on us while he tied our hands and feet. Right then I knew how mashed potatoes feel.

The Gila monster hung us by our tails from the high dive.

"Bye-bye, Gecko and bird," he said. "When they find you—too late. I will have my revenge."

"Hang in there," Nadine snickered.

They left. We hung upside down, like a couple of bats. My stomach growled and I daydreamed about spicy red fire ants in cream sauce.

"Well, look on the bright side," said Natalie. "It could be worse."

I gave her a disgusted look. "How?"

"He could have turned on the automatic pool chlorinator."

A switch clicked somewhere in the building. A deep humming was followed by the hiss of something bubbling through the pool's filters.

The smell made my eyes water. Chlorine gas.

"Thanks a lot, Natalie," I said.

18

Hanging by a Tail

We coughed and blinked our watery eyes as the chlorine gas bubbled in the pool below. What a way to go—slowly stunk to death.

"So, about our partnership," said Natalie. She knew I wasn't going anywhere. "Is this a good time to talk?"

"All right, all right!" I said. "I guess... you can be my partner—if we ever get out of here."

"That's great, Chet! Thanks."

I grunted. "Don't mention it."

We watched the pool bubble and the sun crawl lower in the sky out the window. A big clock ticked on the wall, counting down the minutes to Herman's revenge.

From the football field came a sound like a porcupine sitting on a bagpipe. The band was tuning up. Or maybe that was their first number; I couldn't tell.

"Hey, Chet," said Natalie. "As long as we're just hanging here, let's finish solving the mystery."

"Good idea. So . . . we know Herman is going to do something with his 'little friends' to disrupt the game." I furrowed my brow. "What else did he say?"

"The kickoff is the first surprise," said Natalie. "Now, what could be so surprising about a kickoff?"

I coughed on the chlorine fumes. "Well, they could steal the football."

"Nah," she said. "Too easy. And the team could get another ball."

My mind flashed on Herman's visit to the dump. "What if they switched the ball?" I said. "Maybe Herman made an exploding ball with stuff they found at the dump."

Natalie and I looked at each other. "Nah," we said together.

Herman couldn't make toast without an instruction book. It had to be something simpler.

"Garbage!" I said. "He filled a football with garbage, and it's going to get all over the team when they kick off."

"Now we're cooking!" said Natalie. She gave me an upside-down grin. "Chet, you do some serious thinking when the blood runs to your head. You should do your homework upside down."

"Never mind the compliments," I said. "Let's solve the rest of this. There was an *M* on Billy's map—*M* for mashed potatoes? *M* for muffins?"

Natalie turned in her ropes. The movement made her swing slowly in circles. "Chet, get your mind off food!"

"M-m-m-mascot! It's the school mascot. Now, what was it Herman said?"

Natalie's eyes grew big. "Even the mascot would wish it had never been born. Oh, Chet! Do you think Herman's going to destroy our Golden Gopher?"

"That ugly statue? I'd help him."

"Chet!" Natalie huffed.

"I'm kidding, I'm kidding. You're right, Natalie. He's going to grab the statue while everyone's distracted." I twisted my arms against the ropes. "Now if only we could get out of here, we could stop Herman and free Billy."

"Well, partner." Natalie sighed. "Looks like Herman wins this round."

I hated to admit it, but she was right. We were hanging from the diving board and choking on chlorine instead of sticking right to Herman's tail.

Wait a minute!

"Not so fast," I said. "He may be strong, but he's no smart cookie. Herman forgot one thing."

"What's that?" she asked.

"We geckos have a secret weapon."

And with that, I detached my tail and splashed down into the pool.

19

Revenge on the Fifty-Yard Line

Given a choice, most geckos would rather visit the dentist than go swimming. I wriggled out of that overchlorinated pool fast as I could, and crawled to Coach Stroganoff's office. I sawed off the ropes on my hands and feet with his letter opener.

Leave it to Hicky Elementary to have a coach so tough he uses a steak knife as a letter opener.

"Quick, Chet!" said Natalie. "Get me out of here. The game's about to start."

She was right. We could hear the marching band playing its last song. Or maybe they were beating it to death. It was hard to tell the difference.

The team would kick off any minute now. I climbed the high dive and began hacking at the rope holding Natalie's tail.

"Wait a second," said Natalie. "Don't cut *that* rope, you bug brain—I'll drown if I fall. Cut the rope around my wings first."

"Hey, who you calling bug brain? Remember who's holding the knife."

"Chet, please!"

Hanging by my feet from the diving board, I could just reach the rope around her wings. I stretched my arm to its fullest and sawed at the rope. When it gave, Natalie stretched her wings suddenly.

The knife was knocked from my hand and slipped into the stinky pool. *Splash!*

"Smooth move!" I said. "Now look what you've done."

"Hurry, Chet! Get me out of here!"

She managed to untie her feet using her beak. I fumbled with the remaining knots and finally untied Natalie's tail.

Natalie fell like a sack of birdseed, then spread her wings, just skimming the pool's surface. She landed poolside.

With one sad look back, I left my old tail hanging from the diving board. I'd start growing another one in a week or so.

"Wow, you look weird," said Natalie.

"This ain't no beauty contest, sister," I said. "Now take me up on your back and let's fly out to that field."

For once, she didn't argue.

I hopped onto her back. Natalie flapped heavily out toward the football field. We swerved, almost creaming a tall trash can.

"Watch out!" I said.

Her belly feathers scraped a low fence. Coming in under the trees, she almost lost me on a scraggly branch. The field was just ahead.

"Faster, Natalie!"

The band made one last blast, like a water buffalo losing its lunch.

The song was over. The game was about to begin.

I spotted Herman and his gang under the bleachers.

"Drop me off here," I told Natalie. "I'll handle their 'little friends.' You get that garbage football."

"Be careful," she said.

"You, too, partner."

Natalie grinned and took off. I ran across the end zone.

A short green referee with bad hair gave our quarterback the football. The referee looked familiar. But I had no time for guessing games.

"Chester Gecko!" a voice shouted. "Come here this instant!"

It was Ms. Glick, beside the bleachers. She was not a happy gator.

I looked back at the field. Our team was kicking off. The center hiked the ball, and the quarterback caught it. He planted the football.

The kicker ran toward it, and the whole team began running with him. The crowd jumped to its feet and roared.

"Go, Natalie!" I shouted.

Natalie flapped her heart out. The kicker, a beefy chipmunk, charged the football. When he booted it, the ball would burst into a million pieces of stinky garbage—all over the team.

Everything seemed to move in slow motion.

Flap, flap! went Natalie's wings. The kicker's legs pumped. The crowd chanted, "Gophers! Gophers!" And Ms. Glick snarled as she strode toward me.

Just before the chipmunk's foot hit the ball, Natalie swooped low and snatched it from under the quarterback's fingers.

"Hey!" he said. "That's our ball!"

Natalie flapped across the field and over the bleachers. From the crowd, hands reached for her and missed. She dumped the ball in a trash can.

A small fountain of funky garbage—brown bananas, rotten cheese, and rancid mothloaf—shot skyward as the ball burst.

I looked back at the field . . .

And ducked fast as Ms. Glick grabbed at me. I dodged under her leathery arms and beat feet up the sidelines.

Herman and the short referee were dragging the wriggly sack from under the bleachers. The referee's wig slipped. Then I knew: It was Billy! Helping Herman!

They were still trying to pull off Part 2 of Herman's prank.

I ran toward them.

"Too late, tough guy!" sneered Herman. He stood with feet planted wide and crowed in triumph.

The Gila monster opened the sack. And out poured a brown stream of giant cockroaches, headed straight for the football field.

20

Roaches "R" Us

Too late! I couldn't stop Herman. I could only watch as wave upon wave of cockroaches raced from that sack onto the grass.

The mice and other rodent players squealed. They milled in confusion. The lizards on the team looked hungrily at the brown wave.

Herman would snatch the mascot while everyone was busy with the cockroaches. But not if I could help it.

My stomach rumbled like a volcano. And then it hit me.

Lunchtime!

I shot onto the field and dodged between the players. I grabbed handful after handful of delicious cockroaches. *Crunch, crunch!* I slowed down only to spit out the wings and feet.

I munched those bugs like it was the final event in the Lunchtime Olympics.

It wasn't a pretty sight.

I got so involved with my long-delayed lunch, I forgot about the last part of Herman's plan. The mascot! I searched for the Gila monster among the crowd of feasting lizards, scurrying cockroaches, and squeaking rodents.

Even the spectators had joined the free-for-all on the field. It was a madhouse. I staggered past a skink and a newt playing tug-of-war with a cockroach.

On the sidelines, the cheerleaders were continuing their routine. They tossed the other team's mascot—the Big Baboo—up into the air, then stomped on it. The girls cheered happily.

I shook my head. I'd hate to make a cheerleader mad at me.

"I'll get you, Chester Gecko!" shouted Ms. Glick, as a tide of hefty football players trompled over her. I turned, scanning the crowd for a no-good Gila monster.

Finally I spotted him.

Herman had tucked the Golden Gopher statue under his arm like a football. He was running for the end zone and freedom!

I was too full to run. But I couldn't let him escape. I staggered and tripped. *Oof!* I hit the ground. Herman was getting away.

In desperation, I rolled and zapped out my tongue. It stuck to the goalpost at ankle height—right in Herman's path.

Too late. He saw me. His eyes went wide.

Ba-tonk!

Herman tripped on my tongue and went down like mowed grass. The Golden Gopher flew from his hands and landed—*whump!*—right on my stomach.

Normally it would've hurt. But I was so stuffed, I couldn't feel a thing. I could barely move.

Coach Stroganoff parted the tide of football players and spectators. He stood over me.

"Nice catch, Gecko!" he said. "I saw the whole thing."

He grabbed the statue in one hand and hoisted Herman by the tail with the other. Coach Stroganoff slung the Gila monster over his back.

"Mister, you're in deep doo-doo," he said to Herman. The Gila monster just groaned. Coach Stroganoff took a couple of steps, then turned back to me.

"You know, Gecko, we could use someone like you on our football team. Let me know when you reach sixth grade."

I grunted. My tongue felt like the elastic on your oldest pair of underwear.

From my comfortable spot on the grass, I watched Coach Stroganoff drag Herman away. Maybe the Gila monster would beat my detention record. Maybe they'd lock him up and throw away the key.

Right then, I didn't care. I had a full belly, and a case that was almost wrapped up.

If that's not heaven, what is?

21

Just Desserts

Across the field, I saw Ms. Glick being carried off by the crowd. When she woke up, she'd give me enough pink slips to wallpaper a house. Ah, well. I live for danger.

Shirley ran up to me in her little cheerleader skirt.

"Chet! You didn't find my brother, and I'm in big trouble!"

"Guess again, sister," I said. "Check out that referee."

Shirley shoved her way through the crowd and grabbed the short referee. She tore his hair off—a wig! As I had thought, it was her brother, Billy.

I couldn't hear her words, but I saw Billy turn a lovely shade of red.

She dragged him over to me as Natalie landed beside us on the grass.

"Some detective you are!" said Shirley. "You didn't find him until the very last minute." She looked me up and down, then smiled. "But I guess you tried your best."

She kissed me on the cheek.

"Gross!" said her brother.

What was I, some kind of cootie magnet? I'll never understand dames.

"You look pretty funny." Shirley chuckled. "With no tail and that big belly, you look just like a bullfrog."

"Ha-ha," I tried to say. But I was so stuffed, all that came out was a loud *"Buuurp!"*

"You sound like a frog, too," said Shirley.

"Hey, that's my partner you're talking about," said Natalie.

I gave them both my best tough-guy look. But my belly was so heavy, I didn't dare open my mouth again.

"So, Billy, how did Herman make you go along with his prank?" said Natalie. "What cruel blackmail did he use?"

"Blackmail?!" said Billy. "I would have *paid* him to let me help. I hate that stupid gopher mascot. Our mascot should be a lizard."

Natalie and I looked at each other. He had a point there.

"*Buurp*—but what about that drawing I saw in your desk?" I said.

"You were looking at my comic strip?" said Billy. He ducked his head.

"And why did you get mad when Herman was joking about your sister yesterday?" said Natalie.

Billy's eyes spun in their sockets. "He told me he caught Shirley writing *Shirley + Chet = love 4 ever* on a wall. That makes me sick. It's totally gross!"

I had to agree with him.

No wonder Shirley didn't tell me she was a cheerleader. She didn't want me to know that she knew Herman, and that he knew her mushy secret.

"Did you know Herman was planning his revenge?" Natalie asked.

Shirley turned a delicate shade of scarlet and cleared her throat. "Kind of," she said in a small voice. "But he said he wouldn't tell my secret if I wouldn't tell his."

Shirley studied some clouds above us like they were going to be on the next science test. Natalie smirked and wiggled her eyebrows. I shook my head in disgust.

Shirley cleared her throat again. "Look, fair's fair. You found Billy, so I'll keep my part of the bargain. Tomorrow morning, expect a great big piece of stinkbug pie."

Stinkbug pie?! Right then, I was too full even to think about it. But, as every detective knows, tomorrow is another case.

Would *you* rescue *your* principal? Chet would.
Find out why in
The Mystery of Mr. Nice

I looked around the waiting room. Strange. Where a line of smart alecks usually sat waiting for justice, empty chairs greeted me.

Principal Zero must be putting his punishment on speed dial, I thought.

I stepped inside. Behind a wide black desk sat Principal Zero, the source of all discipline at Emerson Hicky Elementary. I knew I was about to get mine.

"Yes?" he said.

I laid my pink slip and the torn drawing side by side on his desk. He looked from one to the other.

"Nice artwork, Mr. . . . Gecko," he said. "It has a wonderful sense of color, and the style is quite mature."

I blinked. He was serious.

"Lovely use of dark and light," said Principal Zero. He picked up the pink slip. "Now, what seems to be the problem?"

"Well, Mr. Ratnose didn't . . . um . . . like my drawing."

"I can't believe it," he said. "Perhaps his taste in art is not so refined. I'd love to have a piece like this in my collection. Could you bear to part with it?"

That's when I knew.

Either my principal had lost his mind, or someone had kidnapped the real Mr. Zero.

And coming soon—more mysteries from the Tattered Casebook of Chet Gecko

Case #3 *Farewell, My Lunchbag*

If danger is my business, then dinner is my passion. I'll take any case if the pay is right. And what pay could be better than Mothloaf Surprise?

At least that's what I thought. But in this particular case I bit off more than I could chew.

Cafeteria lady Mrs. Bagoong hired me to track down whoever was stealing her food supplies. The long, slimy trail led too close to my own backyard for comfort.

And much, much too close to my old archenemy, Jimmy "King" Cobra. Without the help of Natalie Attired and our school janitor, Maureen DeBree, I would've been gecko sushi.

Case #4 *The Big Nap*

My grades were lower than a salamander's slippers, and my bank account was trying to crawl under a duck's belly. So why did I take a case that didn't pay anything?

Put it this way: Would *you* stand by and watch some evil power turn *your* classmates into hypnotized zombies? (If that wasn't just what normally happened to them in math class, I mean.)

My investigations revealed a plot meaner than a roomful of rhinos with diaper rash.

Someone at Emerson Hicky was using a sinister video game to put more and more students into la-la-land. And it was up to me to stop it, pronto—before that someone caught up with me, and I found myself taking the Big Nap.

Case #5 *The Hamster of the Baskervilles*

Elementary school is a wild place. But this was ridiculous.

Someone—or some*thing*—was tearing up Emerson Hicky. Classrooms were trashed. Walls were gnawed. Mysterious tunnels riddled the playground like worm chunks in a pan of earthworm lasagna.

But nobody could spot the culprit, let alone catch him.

I don't believe in the supernatural. My idea of voodoo is my mom's cockroach ripple ice cream.

Then a teacher reported seeing a monster on full-moon night, and I got the call.

At the end of a twisted trail of clues, I had to answer the burning question: Was it a vicious, supernatural were-hamster on the loose, or just another Science Fair project gone wrong?

And coming soon—more mysteries from the Tattered Casebook of Chet Gecko

Case #3 *Farewell, My Lunchbag*

If danger is my business, then dinner is my passion. I'll take any case if the pay is right. And what pay could be better than Mothloaf Surprise?

At least that's what I thought. But in this particular case I bit off more than I could chew.

Cafeteria lady Mrs. Bagoong hired me to track down whoever was stealing her food supplies. The long, slimy trail led too close to my own backyard for comfort.

And much, much too close to my old archenemy, Jimmy "King" Cobra. Without the help of Natalie Attired and our school janitor, Maureen DeBree, I would've been gecko sushi.

Case #4 *The Big Nap*

My grades were lower than a salamander's slippers, and my bank account was trying to crawl under a duck's belly. So why did I take a case that didn't pay anything?

Put it this way: Would *you* stand by and watch some evil power turn *your* classmates into hypnotized zombies? (If that wasn't just what normally happened to them in math class, I mean.)

My investigations revealed a plot meaner than a roomful of rhinos with diaper rash.

Someone at Emerson Hicky was using a sinister video game to put more and more students into la-la-land. And it was up to me to stop it, pronto—before that someone caught up with me, and I found myself taking the Big Nap.

Case #5 *The Hamster of the Baskervilles*

Elementary school is a wild place. But this was ridiculous.

Someone—or some*thing*—was tearing up Emerson Hicky. Classrooms were trashed. Walls were gnawed. Mysterious tunnels riddled the playground like worm chunks in a pan of earthworm lasagna.

But nobody could spot the culprit, let alone catch him.

I don't believe in the supernatural. My idea of voodoo is my mom's cockroach ripple ice cream.

Then a teacher reported seeing a monster on full-moon night, and I got the call.

At the end of a twisted trail of clues, I had to answer the burning question: Was it a vicious, supernatural were-hamster on the loose, or just another Science Fair project gone wrong?

Case #6 *This Gum for Hire*

Never thought I'd see the day when one of my worst enemies would hire me for a case. Herman the Gila Monster was a sixth-grade hoodlum with a first-rate left hook. He told me someone was disappearing the football team, and he had to put a stop to it. Big whoop. He told me he was being blamed for the kidnappings, and he had to clear his name. Boo hoo.

Then he said that I could either take the case and earn a nice reward, or have my face rearranged like a bargain-basement Picasso painted by a spastic chimp.

I took the case.

But before I could find the kidnapper, I had to go undercover. And that meant facing something that scared me worse than a chorus line of criminals in steel-toed boots: P.E. class.